The Same Inside

Other poetry titles from
Macmillan Children's Books

Reaching the Stars
Poems about Extraordinary Women and Girls
Jan Dean, Liz Brownlee and Michaela Morgan

1066 and Before That
History Poems
Brian Moses and Roger Stevens

The Same Inside

Liz Brownlee,
Matt Goodfellow
and
Roger Stevens

Poems about
Empathy
and
Friendship

MACMILLAN
CHILDREN'S
BOOKS

First published 2018 by Macmillan Children's Books
an imprint of Pan Macmillan
20 New Wharf Road, London N1 9RR
Associated companies throughout the world
www.panmacmillan.com

ISBN 978-1-5098-5450-9

1 3 5 7 9 8 6 4 2

A CIP catalogue record for this book is available from
the British Library.

Printed and bound by CPI Group (UK) Ltd, Croydon CR0 4YY

Contents

The Same Inside

Red perfumed apples
and crunchy, crisp green,
used straight from the tree
or in tasty cuisine,
like honey nut charoset
and pies with ice cream.

In Fujis from Co-ops
and Cox's from Spar,
or Java apples
from far Zanzibar;
look inside any apple
and there is a star!

Liz Brownlee

What's My Name?

I'm the sun that lights the playground before
the work begins
I'm the smile when teacher cracks a joke. I'm
the giggles and the grins
In assembly I'm the trophy that the winning
team collects
In your maths book I'm the page of sums
where every one's correct
I'm the pure blue sky and leafy green that
wins the prize in art
I'm steamy, creamy custard dribbling down
the cook's jam tart
I'm the noise of playtime rising through the
stratosphere
I'm the act of kindness when you lent your
kit to Mia
I'm the star you were awarded for your
startling poetry
I'm the school gates swinging open on the
stroke of half past three

If you look for me, you'll find me. What's my name? Can you guess?
I live just round the corner and my name is happiness

Roger Stevens

Being Human

So many pupils in our school
So many hands to hold
So many languages spoken
All with stories to be told

So many ways to look at life
So many jokes and laughs
So many dreams to follow
All with different paths

So many journeys started
All out for a happy end
So many types of human
So many words for friend

Liz Brownlee

Fingerprints

I try to find where mine
begin and end

frustratedly, I check
those of my friend

she watches, gentle-eyed
starts to speak:

don't try to understand
what is unique

Matt Goodfellow

Puzzle

we are

all
jigsaw pieces

before
we
are gone

we
must
find
a
way

to
fit
together
as

one

Matt Goodfellow

Each and Every One

dwi dynol

jeg er menneske

ako ay tao

he tangata ahau

jestem człowiekiem

i ahay aadanaha

ich bin menschlich

abụ m mmadụ

soy humano

sono umano

je suis humain

i am human

Matt Goodfellow

Pyramids

each pyramid you'll find is a square
if you view it from under the base

and a triangle seen from the side
if you're looking at only one face

how many pyramids would you miss
if you viewed them from only one place?

Liz Brownlee

I Don't Care Blues

I don't care if you're black or white
Or any shade between the two
I don't care if you're black or white
Brown, or pink, or even blue
Just remember we're all human beings
That's all you have to do

I don't care if you're a girl who likes boys
Or a boy who likes girls, as many do
I don't care if you're a girl who likes girls
Or a boy who likes boys, that's cool too
Because really it's none of my business
Who you like is really up to you

I don't care if you're from a poor family
Birds got nothing, but they sing
I don't care if you're wealthy
If your mum wears a diamond ring
Cos you know it's the love in your heart
That's the most important thing

Roger Stevens

The blues is a musical form that began in the Deep South of the United States around the end of the nineteenth century. It usually took the form of a loose narrative, often relating the troubles experienced in African-American society.

Can't Take the Future Out of Me

can't take the stars out of the sky
can't take the story from a tree
can't take the moonlight from your eyes
can't take the future out of me

can't take the bark out of a dog
can't take the wildness from the sea
can't take the darkness from a dream
can't take the future out of me

can't take the sparkle from the frost
can't take the bumble from a bee
can't take the pride out of a smile
can't take the future out of me

Matt Goodfellow

Differences of Opinion

Jo likes yellow
I love blue,
but all the same
we're friends, us two.

I'd like a cat
that purrs and stalks,
she wants a dog
to take on walks.

I do breast stroke
Jo does crawl,
I sing in choir
she plays football.

She is busy
every minute,
that competition?
She will win it.

I like dreaming
snuggling, reading,
to call me active
is misleading.

She loves maths –
and Doctor Who,
I love art
and Scooby-Doo.

Jo does homework
double quick . . .
she likes things tidy,
ordered, ticked.

My head is always
in a whirl,
I'm a last-minute
sort of girl.

She thinks 'sensible'
is cool –
I prefer
to play the fool!

Though there's one thing
we do agree . . .
I like Jo
and Jo likes me!

Liz Brownlee

Accident Prone

Joe jumped on my kite
(from the top of the wall)
He spoilt my picture
(knocked the water pot over)
He tipped paint on my head
(after he had knocked the water over)
He lost my coat
(when we were exploring the woods)
He ate my crisps
(by mistake, he said.
How can you eat crisps by mistake?)
He punctured my ball
(by throwing it to the neighbour's dog)
But he's my best friend
So I forgive him
(but I do wish he was more careful
sometimes!)

Roger Stevens

A Friend Ship

A friend ship
is a rowing boat
you both row
alternately

A friend ship
is a hovercraft
that skims above
the stormy sea

A friend ship
is a submarine
following
a secret chart

A friend ship
is a sailing boat
borne by the wind
to the harbour's heart

Roger Stevens

Being Sad

When I'm meeting Milly in the park
And Milly doesn't show
When I ask my best friend for a crisp
And my best friend says, No
When I bite into a juicy plum
And the middle has gone bad
Even writing down this poem
Is making me feel sad
So I'll try and think of good things
Maybe that will cheer me up

When we won the rounders tournament
And I went to collect the cup
When we climbed the hill in Wales
And the cloud shadows swept by
When Granny came to tea
And she made us apple pie
When I wrote to my favourite writer
And she wrote me back a letter
It helps to think of good things
Already I feel better

Roger Stevens

Friend

nobody else saw the tears
as they ran through the rain on my cheeks

nobody else knew the fears
had been steadily growing for weeks

nobody else took a stand
and helped to pull me through

nobody else understands
nobody else but you

Matt Goodfellow

Buddy Chair Rules!

Is your best friend away today?
Go and find a buddy chair!

No one wants to come and play?
Go and find a buddy chair!

Have a game to show and share?
Go and find a buddy chair!

There's always someone there to care
at the find a buddy chair!

Liz Brownlee

At some schools a chair is provided for children to sit on if they are lonely. Any child who sees them sitting there goes to invite them to play.

Names

Names from all around the world
Solemn names, names to be sung
Names of the children in our school
Names to roll around the tongue

Jolie, Marzena, Angelique, Estela
Diego, Dobromil, Artemis, Evita
Delia, Bahati, Ekundayo, Maria
Dido, Meshullam, Takumi, Aika

Rachel, Celestyn, Engelbert, Gwendolen
Yoko, India, Blodwedd, Yarona,
Sigmund, Sofia, Florence, Adoria
Abban, Dayo, Fatima, Song

Meifeng means a beautiful wind
Makary, blessed, Changming, bright
Bahati for luck, Osamare, a rainbow,
Udo for peace, Leokadia, light

Astrid, Steven, Cadence, Jill
Aziz, Fabia, Aliya, Dakota
Magnus, Basma, Amber, Farah,
Jiao, Halona, Nadzieja, Hope

Roger Stevens

Jia-Wen's Grandad

Jia-Wen's grandad came into school
to show our class his paintings.

Before he arrived, me and Barney
were moaning: 'He can't even

speak English – what can we learn?'
He sat down, opened his satchel

and passed his pictures around.
Our fingers traced along strong

black horizons. Hands swept across
mountain peaks, through neat

little villages and over glittering oceans.
I stared into the eyes of a snarling dragon

surrounded by flames. Jia-Wen's grandad
never even spoke. Just packed up his
pictures

gave Jia-Wen a kiss – and was gone.
That night, lying in bed, I heard

wind chimes in bamboo forests, watched
thin smoke-wisps melt into stars

and somewhere deep
in the distance of my dreams

I fire-danced with dragons.

Matt Goodfellow

Together
An Assembly Poem

together we join to celebrate
together we clap and cheer
together we watch improvements
and face the things we fear

together we grow and develop
together we all belong
together we make mistakes
and learn about right and wrong

together we praise the gentle
the kind, the strong, the brave
together we share achievement
in a thousand different ways

together we'll finish the journey
wherever it started from
together we are tomorrow
together we are one

Matt Goodfellow

Teacher

Educator – helps teach you
Narrator – reads books too
Debater – sees both sides
Inspirer – makes you fly
Collaborator – helps you work
Motivator – won't let you shirk!
Appreciator – of what you've done
Surpriser – makes it fun
Creator – builds displays
Arbitrator – finds a way
Liberator – sets minds free
Communicator – helps you see
Demonstrator – shows you how
Confiscator – won't allow
Caretaker – soothes your pain
Mind maker – expands your brain
Respect achiever – respects you
In you believer – you're a star too!

Liz Brownlee

Susan Gets Up

Susan gets up
and extends her hand
the hand that will
pat, fold, unfold
her two white socks

to quiet the whispers
before she puts them on

pat, gently three times
with fingers flat
fold exact
like origami
crease the edge
unfold with care

to quiet the whispers
quiet, quiet,
she is safe now
she whispers back

before she pats
and puts her sandals
side by side
and puts them on
and off, and on

to quiet the whispers
quiet, quiet,
she is safe now
she whispers back

and eats her breakfast
and leaves for school
and calls bye Mum
and whispers

you're safe now

Liz Brownlee

If you are troubled by repetitive thoughts, feelings you must repeat actions, count or collect items or similar to keep yourself or someone you love safe, please tell someone who cares about you, a teacher or a friend.

Promise

I do not believe
and I don't
understand

but when you're in need
I will offer
my hand

Matt Goodfellow

The Most Important Rap

I am an astronaut
I circle the stars
I walk on the moon
I travel to Mars
I'm brave and tall
There is nothing I fear
and I am the most important person here.

I am a teacher
I taught you it all
I taught you why your
spaceship doesn't fall
If you couldn't read or write
where would you be?
The most important person here is me.

Who are you kidding?
Are you taking the mick?
Who makes you better
when you're feeling sick?
I am a doctor
and I'm always on call
and I am more important than you all.

But I'm your mother
Don't forget me
If it wasn't for your mother
where would you be?
I washed your nappies
and changed your vest
I'm the most important
and Mummy knows best.

I am a child
and the future I see
and there'd be no future
if it wasn't for me
I hold the safety
of the planet in my hand
I'm the most important
and you'd better understand.

Now just hold on
I've a message for you all
Together we stand
and divided we fall
So let's make a circle
and all remember this
Who's the most important?

EVERYBODY IS!

Roger Stevens

Beware the Bytes

Digital storage
it hums, buzzes, whirrs
with the binary codes
of the world's words

Each picture posted
each thought on screen
on social media
is recorded and seen

Billions of bytes
and trillions of codes
monitoring minds
and every download

Infinite internet
knows no wrong or right
displays both regardless –
BEWARE these bytes BITE!

Liz Brownlee

Always be supportive in your internet interactions.
If you are targeted by a bully, take a screengrab or
photo for evidence, unfriend the culprit, block them,
report them.

Choices

bitter words:

> gloat
>
> killed

better words:

> vote
>
> build

bitter words:

> greed
>
> scare

better words:
>   feed
>   share

bitter words:
>   scream
>   shove

better words:
>   dream
>   love

Matt Goodfellow

The Girls

the dread of whispers
I'm scared to hear
but want to hear
the sideways looks

the words that hurt
like bruises
the lies
that scald

what have I done?
is it my fault?
the giggles
the smirks

can someone tell me
what works?

Liz Brownlee

Circle of Bullying

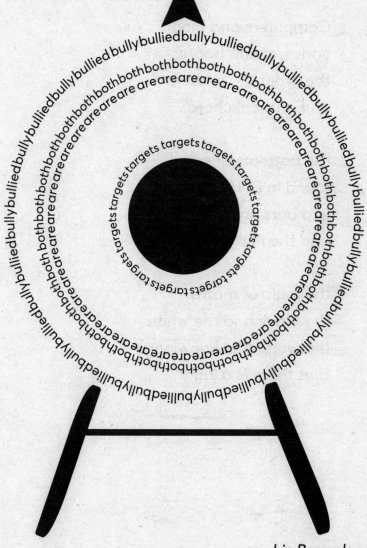

Liz Brownlee

Another Dimension

Computers and binary
codes, circuit boards
the order of numbers
and musical chords

the patterns of spirals
found in DNA
in plants and in pine cones
and the Milky Way

the logic of maths
the black and the white
the wonderful knowledge
that there is a 'right'

the comfort of puzzles
to lose myself in
the fun of the problems
I can't wait to begin

I'm not a square
in a round world; I'm me –
just one dimension of
what it means 'to be'.

Liz Brownlee

A Different Kind of Poem

a different kind of poem
might be short, long
or somewhere in between

a different kind of poem
might chime with rhyme
or it might not

a different kind of poem
might have an unconventional and seemingly
    ungainly rhythm
making it flow quite differently from those you
    are used to

a different kind of poem
                might
pattern   the   page   how
        it
wants   to
entirely   disregarding   what

any   other   poem   is
doing

a different kind of poem
might discuss issues
that you find awkward or
uncomfortable

a different kind of poem
might do some, none
or all of the above
but

a different kind of poem
is still
a poem

isn't it?

Matt Goodfellow

Judge Me

judge me by my actions
    not the colour of my skin

judge me by achievement
    and the friendships that I win

judge me by the life I lead,
    decisions that I make

judge me by the things I say
    and hands I choose to shake

judge me as an equal –
    call me by my name

judge me when you realize:
    inside we are the same

Matt Goodfellow

Longing for Wide Open Spaces

Do you ever feel
As if the world
Is closing in?
Asif thereis notime tothink?
Asyouwalk alongthestreet
Peoplejostleandpush you
And you want to shout
Givemeroomtobreathe
Andyoudreamofclamberinghighhills
In the wide open countryside
Just   y o u

alone   with   the

s   k   y

Roger Stevens

Rise

The end of our school field
where the grass grows long
is where I sometimes hide
when the world is going wrong

I lie among the dandelions
staring at the sky
wishing I was someone else
wishing I could fly

out into the atmosphere
swooping through the clouds
somewhere much less complicated
somewhere much less loud

somewhere safe and peaceful
where all secrets are revealed
I close my eyes, become the skies
and rise above this field

Matt Goodfellow

My Sister Is a Rainbow

my sister is a rainbow
beautiful and bold
everybody watches her
and leaves me in the cold

but they don't know my secret
(you're the only one I've told):
my sister is a rainbow
but I'm the pot of gold

Matt Goodfellow

The Only Way

alThough
yOu and I
beLieve different things
wE must
always Respect
eAch other's right
to live iN
peaCe
forevEr

Matt Goodfellow

Boy or Girl?

Two Tricky Riddles

1
You love your teddy bear
You love wearing cool clothes
Your favourite colour is pink
What are you?

2
You love to rough and tumble
You love football
Your favourite colour is blue
What are you?

Answers:
1. Either
2. Either

Roger Stevens

In the Woods

walking in the woods
I am a thousand different things
I am rain-shine on a beech bud
I'm the song a blackbird sings

I am pollen in a sunbeam
I'm an ash leaf's falling spin
I'm a patch of slender grasses
shadow-dancing in the wind

I'm an acorn in the bramble
I am rising river mist
I am blossom on a blackthorn
I am all I ever wished

Matt Goodfellow

Help Available

If you're feeling vexed
    Send me a text
If you've got the glums
    Ring up your chums
If you're feeling blue
    Make a phone call or two
If you're not feeling great
    Call up a mate
Want the blues to end?
    Chat with a friend
Too much to take?
    Then we'll go down to the beach
    and have a yummy ice cream with
    a chocolate flake

Roger Stevens

Prayer

I'm never too busy for fairy tales
I'm never too busy for games
I'm never too busy for singing a song
or making a den when it rains

I'm never too busy for rainbows
I'm never too busy for dreams
I'm never too busy for frightening friends
and filling a room with their screams

I'm never too busy for birthdays
I'm never too busy to cry
I'm never too busy to stare at the stars
that glitter a clear summer sky

I'm never too busy for sprinkles
or chocolate ice cream after tea
I'm never too busy to say what I think
and hope that I never will be

Matt Goodfellow

Circle of Life

The aphids and the tiny ants
that run the teeming, gleaming plants
are eaten by the shiny frogs
which nestle under leaves and logs.

The flies and irritating gnats
are snatched in flight by swooping bats,
and any insects on the wing
are gulped where glitzy lizards cling.

Chimps eat piles of juicy fruits
leave seeds that grow into the shoots
of trees which give the forest trails,
and monkey swings for arms and tails;

a place for tiger's quiet pace,
and space for leopard's hunt and chase.
Each species in the world alive
needs all the others to survive.

And everyone on planet Earth
has consequence, talent and worth,
animals and humans too –
a role for me, and one for you.

Liz Brownlee

Brave

When Dad and Mum cannot agree
And I am on my own again
I sit beneath this twisted tree
And shelter from the rain

The sky is black, the lightning white
I watch the weather misbehave
I wonder, are birds scared of thunder?
And if so, are they brave?

Roger Stevens

Night Puzzle

can I sleep with those words going round and round my head and why did you say those words you said and how

Roger Stevens

I'm Sorry

As I lie here in bed
These words swim in my head
I'm sorry

Our head teacher said
That words can't be unsaid
I'm sorry

I called you maggot pie
I said I hope you die
I'm sorry

I'm sorry for today
Tomorrow I will say
I'm sorry

Roger Stevens

Forgiveness

I've seen a broken vase
mended carefully before
that looked if not more beautiful
as good despite its flaw

your nice apology
and me forgiving you
will make our friendship stronger
though we have a crack or two!

Liz Brownlee

Just Like Me

Are your bones white?
Is your blood red?
Do you breathe air?

Does your brain think?
Do you daydream?
Are you aware?

Do you wake up?
Do you sleep?
Does your heart beat?

Do you get thirsty?
And feel hungry?
Do you have to eat?

Do you smile?
Do you love?
Do you need a friend?

Feel happiness?
And sadness?
Long for war to end?

Do you cry?
Do you laugh?
Do you wish to be free?

Then though I
am in a wheelchair,
you are just like me.

Liz Brownlee

Get on the Team (of Life)

We need:

leaders and readers
and help-those-in-need-ers
to join in together
and get on the team

wavers and savers
and those-who-amaze-us
to join in together
and get on the team

healers, believers
and keeping-it-real-ers
to join in together
and get on the team

carers and sharers
and hands-in-the-air-ers
to join in together
and get on the team

grinners and winners
and want-to-begin-ers
to join in together
and get on the team

friend-ers and menders
and stay-till-the-end-ers
to join in together
and get on the team

dreamers and schemers
and all-inbetween-ers
so what are you waiting for?
Get on the team!

Matt Goodfellow

Speaking and Listening

'If speaking is silver, then listening is gold.'
Turkish proverb

Speaking is a bowl of soup
Listening is a spoon
Speaking is a cloudy sky
Listening is the moon
Speaking is an empty plate
Listening is a sausage roll
Speaking is a clever pass
Listening is a goal
Speaking is a cycle wheel
Listening is a tyre

Speaking is a wintry wind
Listening is a cosy fire
Speaking is a diving board
Listening is diving
Speaking is a long car drive
Listening is arriving
Speaking is a monologue
Listening is a cabaret
If you speak and never listen
What will you have to say?

Roger Stevens

Luck

When I'm thirsty
there's the tap

water flows
just like that

in Angola
instead of play

to fetch a drink
I'd walk all day

Liz Brownlee

To This

I came with nothing
but the Mediterranean in my eyes
and a knot in my stomach

to this

concrete chaos
rainy streets
icy looks
burning cheeks

Dad
on the balcony
waving
as we
drove away

to this
to this

Matt Goodfellow

Listening to Nan

she looked at me
and smiled
as she untied
her pinny.
you see, she said,
life's just like
the dot to dots
in that book
of yours:
you start
at the first one
and just keep
moving on
hoping you'll
find the next
without making
too much mess.
and then
all of a sudden

you find your
last dot

and that's
your

lot

Matt Goodfellow

Refugee

After the bombing
and all are lost
and gone

I walk

I can carry only
my father's pride
my mother's longing
my brother's blood
my sister's hope
and my dreams

but my father's pride
cannot be carried
as a refugee
so I lay it down

and I walk

when I sleep
my mother's longing
is too painful to hold
so I lay it down

and I walk

until my shoes
fall off my feet
and I leave
my brother's blood
and my own
on the road
as if it is worthless

and I walk
so far and
sleep so little
I cannot remember
my dreams

I can carry only
my sister's hope
which is light

in my heart

Liz Brownlee

Farewell

If the final farewell
Could have been planned
You would have said,
'I'll miss you. Please don't go.'

You would have held her hand
One final time.
You would have tried
To unfound her fears.

Instead Mum gets a phone call.
And you walk into the garden all alone
To watch the blur of butterflies
Through tears

Roger Stevens

Let Our Light Shine

Oh, vast and marvellous universe
may your suns shine in all of us
let one and all humanity
live in perfect unity
give us kind hearts and gentle hands
to love what we don't understand
stir the earth within us; from that springs
compassion for each living thing
know we are only from our birth
one silk in the web of life on Earth
help truth unravel hate and lies
join our hearts with simple ties
for our lovely planet's sake
may we return more than we take
don't let wrongdoing have its day
because we looked the other way
let our light shine on and on
in peace and trust and love and song.

Liz Brownlee

About Liz Brownlee

Liz Brownlee loves wildlife, the subject of her book *Animal Magic* (Iron Press). She's also written *Reaching for the Stars: Poems about Extraordinary Women and Girls* (Macmillan), with Jan Dean and Michaela Morgan, and *Apes to Zebras: an A–Z of Shape Poems* (Bloomsbury), with Sue Hardy-Dawson and Roger Stevens.

Liz does readings and workshops on all the above books, with her assistance dog, Lola, at schools, libraries, literary and nature festivals. She has fun organizing poetry retreats, exhibitions and events, and runs the poetry website Poetry Roundabout. She is a National Poetry Day Ambassador.

About Matt Goodfellow

Matt Goodfellow is a poet and primary school teacher from Manchester. His most recent collection of poems, *Carry Me Away*, was published in 2016. He spends half his week as a teacher – and the other half touring the UK, visiting schools, libraries and festivals to deliver high-energy, inspirational poetry performances and workshops. He is a National Poetry Day Ambassador.

To book Matt for an event at your school, library or festival, you can contact him at mattgoodfellowpoet@hotmail.com

About Roger Stevens

Roger Stevens visits schools, libraries and festivals, performing his work and running workshops for young people and teachers. He is a National Poetry Day Ambassador, a founding member of the Able Writers scheme with Brian Moses and runs the award-winning poetry website www.poetryzone.co.uk for children and teachers. He has published over thirty books of poetry for children. He spends his time between the Loire, in France, and Brighton, where he lives with his wife and a very, very, very shy dog called Jasper.

REACHING THE STARS

POEMS ABOUT Extraordinary WOMEN & GIRLS

JAN DEAN, LIZ BROWNLEE
& MICHAELA MORGAN

Brian Moses and Roger Stevens take you on a whistle-stop tour through history – from the Stone Age to the Battle of Hastings – in this fantastic, informative and witty collection of poems.